E. B. Clark

Twelve Months in Peru

E. B. Clark

Twelve Months in Peru

ISBN/EAN: 9783337382971

Printed in Europe, USA, Canada, Australia, Japan

Cover: Foto ©Andreas Hilbeck / pixelio.de

More available books at **www.hansebooks.com**

TWELVE MONTHS IN PERU

BY

E. B. CLARK

ILLUSTRATED

LONDON

T. FISHER UNWIN

PATERNOSTER SQUARE

1891

PRINTED AT THE EDINBURGH PRESS,
9 AND 11 YOUNG STREET.

TO

MRS. HOWARD JOHNSTON,

OF MIRAFLORES,

WHOSE KINDNESS AND HOSPITALITY AFFORD
THE AUTHORESS SO MANY PLEASANT RECOLLECTIONS OF
HER VISIT TO PERU, THIS SKETCH IS LOVINGLY

DEDICATED

PREFACE.

In presenting this little work to the public, one word of apology is due for its autobiographical tendency.

Far was it from my original purpose to thrust my own individuality so prominently into the foreground — as my historical manuscripts will testify—and the suggestions of those more qualified to judge than my humble self must be responsible for the seeming egotism. Nevertheless I venture to hope that my efforts to please may claim at least a

small portion of that leniency and gene-
rosity that characterise the reading public,
wheresoever they may be and to whatso-
ever nationality they may belong.

E. B. C.

CONTENTS.

FROM COLON TO LIMA.

CHAPTER I.

CHAPTER II.

CHAPTER III.

IN THE SIERRA.

CHAPTER I.

CHAPTER II.

CHAPTER III.

CHAPTER IV.

LIST OF ILLUSTRATIONS.

INTRODUCTION.

As Peruvian annals date no further back
than the eleventh century, our knowledge
of the aborigines of the country must
necessarily be scanty and conjectural to a
very great extent ; and the ancient Egyp-
tians, Assyrians, Chinese, and Asiatic-
Indians have all been quoted by anti-
quarians as probable progenitors of the
great Peruvian-Indian race. But whoever
the earliest inhabitants may have been,

certain it is that they left behind them many valuable and substantial monuments, which their successors, the INCAS, who governed the country for upwards of four hundred years previous to the Spanish Conquest in 1535, were not slow in appreciating and imitating.

Like the warlike Aztecs, Peruvians claimed descent from bearded white men, and what Quetzalcoatl was to the former Manco Capac was to the latter. Both are represented as mysterious beings, appearing without any indication of the places of their birth, and acting as high-priests and legislators, desirous of promoting peace, industry, and the arts, and effecting a sudden change in the policy of both nations, by whom they were received with joy and veneration. The word INCA signified in Quichua a *king* or *lord*, and the office was hereditary. Twelve or thirteen of these Incas reigned in succession from INGASMAN or MANCO CAPAC to ATAHUALPA, whose contentions with his half-brother HUASCAR for universal empire rendered the country so easy a prey to the Spaniards under FRANCISCO PIZARRO, and gave rise to the saying that " whereas the subjugation of the Mexicans required the abilities of a Cortés, that of the gentle and yielding Peruvians needed only the unblushing perfidy and rude daring of a Pizarro." At Cuzco, Huascar's capital, stood that magnificent temple dedicated to the Sun, which has been described as a "mine of burnished gold."

The first intimation the Spaniards had of this southern El Dorado was probably in the year 1511, when, according to the historian Herrera, who derived his information from the sons of the Conquerors, a young barbarian, observing some Spaniards weighing and distributing gold and silver with much avidity, told Vasco Nuñez de Balboa, the Spanish Governor of Darien, that he knew of a land where gold was as plentiful as iron to an European, and where he could eat and drink out of golden vessels. The natural cupidity of the Spaniard was now aroused, and in 1513 he and a few bold men crossed the narrow, and then almost impenetrable, Isthmus which separates the Atlantic and Pacific Oceans, and prepared for an exploring expedition southward; but it was reserved for Francisco Pizarro, one of his followers, to unite the vast Peruvian Empire to the Spanish crown.

Desperate deeds are best wrought by desperate men, and Pizarro's greatest successes were undoubtedly due to his *coups-de-main* in emergencies when most other commanders would have hesitated to risk an offensive measure. For example, his capture of the Inca Atahualpa in the very midst of his followers, and the perfidious death of that unfortunate monarch when De Soto, the future discoverer of the Mississippi, and the only Spaniard who would have dared to raise the voice of justice against the Conqueror's informal act, was absent searching for proof of his imputed guilt in fomenting a rebellion amongst the Indians.

But the exactions and oppressions of the settlers and their descendants at length aroused the latent ire of the Peruvian race ; and when their champion General San Martin arrived with his 3000 Argentines, aided by war-ships and transports from Chili, commanded by Earl Cochrane, they gladly rose *en masse* and proclaimed their independence on July 28th, 1821.

Thus ended Spanish sovereignty in " The Land of the Incas " after an occupaton of about 286 years under forty-three successive Viceroys.

I.

From Colon to Lima.

B

CHAPTER I.

"Your countrymen seem to know but little about our social condition," is a remark that meets the English traveller in South America oftener perhaps than he could wish; and however promptly and unblushingly he may parry the attack by boasting that the British possessions *alone* would demand a long life's study, yet a secret consciousness remains that the taunt is not unfounded, and particularly may this be said with regard to *Peru*, for beyond knowing that it is a country on the west coast of South America noted for silver mines, guano, revolutions, and earthquakes, this most interesting " Land of the Incas" is to the average Englishman a *terra incognita.*

For this reason, and after twelve months' residence in the Republic, I purpose giving my countrymen and women a brief outline of my own experience and observations there, trusting that it may not be uninteresting to them to tread its tropical shores and climb its Andean heights in imagination instead of adopting the more arduous physical process.

Some years ago Fate, Chance, or whatever that mysterious hidden power may be, transplanted me to the Brazilian shores ; and it was during a few months' sojourn there that my first keen interest in the Peruvian Indian race arose. Most gladly, then, did I undertake a journey to Peru in 1889, and personally acquaint myself with this ancient historic land.

With gallant speed our vessel ploughed the mighty deep, and seventeen days from Liverpool approached the wharf of Aspinwall (although I cling to the name *Colon*, and always mourn the fact of the great Columbus dying in ignorance of his achievement—the finding of a continent), where in mist and rain, early one morning in July, we strained our anxious gaze to view that "deadly Isthmus," "the white man's grave," and satisfy ourselves of its pernicious clime.

Colon stands on the Manzanilla Island, and does not commend itself to the visitor as a desirable life-long residence, unless indeed he hope to "shuffle off this mortal coil" with greater haste than Nature otherwise intended.

A motley population, many of them descended from African slaves, some

foreign-looking shops where costly curios-
ities abound, delicious fruits peculiar to the
tropics, and a few good residences facing
the sea, are its most striking features.
While on Monkey Hill close by an
imposing looking cemetery appears, where
the remains of the victims on both Railroad and Canal are laid.

When I say that we did not personally
inspect this cemetery, I quote it as a
remarkable fact, because, as a rule,
visitors are taken to them in South
American towns immediately on landing,
either because they are the best-kept
public walks, or because they aid
reflection, and are conducive to a little
wholesome melancholia I suppose. Spanish, or a dialect of it, is spoken generally
on the Isthmus, and strange enough the
jargon sounds to uninitiated ears. From

May to October is its winter or rainy
season, when malaria prevails to a greater
extent than usual, and the beautiful
flowers and fruits, which at other periods
of the year grow so luxuriantly, refuse
to show their hidden wealth and beauty.
Indeed the botanist, geologist, and natura-
list have one and all an endless scope for
study in these vast primeval forest lands
and swamps.

But I anticipate, and in order to
obtain a glimpse of this prolific field of
nature the railroad must be traversed.

Imagining that there might possibly
be five or six stations between the
termini—Colon and Panamá, forty-seven
and a half miles apart — I ventured to
suggest inquiry, and great indeed was my
surprise on hearing there were *thirty*
odd.

American cars with cow-catching engines are in use, and for passengers and
baggage the charges are enormous, the
directors doubtless making an extra
charge for the malaria and dust collected
on the way.   Hurrying through life is
not encouraged here, and Isthmian laws
forbid much speed, therefore the traveller
may expect to alight at Panamá in two
and a half or three hours after leaving
Colon, with botanic specimens collected
near the different *dépôts* whilst waiting
for the train to start.   It has been said
that every sleeper on that railroad track
was laid at the cost of a workman's life,
and one certainly has ample time for
dwelling on the melancholy circumstance
during transit.   I wonder what effect an
express train travelling at the rate of a
mile a minute would have upon these

sleepy Isthmian folk, who for the most part lounge around their huts, and smoke and chat throughout the live-long day But the laying of a railroad through such rugged mountain ranges and pestilential morasses was a grand and mighty undertaking after all, and we are filled with admiration when we contemplate the skill of the engineers, and the endurance of the workmen who accomplished it.

When North America acquired the territories of Oregon and California, she found that a more convenient means of communication with her new possessions was desirable, and Mr George Law and Mr William Aspinwall secured a strip of land, extending from the Atlantic to the Pacific Ocean, across the narrow Isthmus. Messrs Aspinwall, John Stephens, and Henry Chauncey then contracted with the

government of New Granada for the
construction of a railroad, and Mr Baldwin, an experienced engineer, explored
the proposed route in company with Mr
Stephens.

The line was not to exceed fifty miles
in length, two ports, one on the Atlantic
and the other on the Pacific, were to be
free of duties, and the contract was to
remain in force for forty-nine years,
unless New Granada should wish to
purchase after the lapse of at least
twenty years. Further, a deposit of
120,000 dollars was to be made at the
commencement, and paid back with
interest on the completion of the work
within eight years.

Now the advantages of this railroad
would be manifold; for besides shortening
and facilitating the route to California,

where gold had lately been discovered, it would also open up a quicker passage to Australia, China, and the East.

The Legislature of New York next became interested in the scheme, and in 1849 granted a charter for the formation of a stock company, when 1,000,000 dollars' worth of stock were taken up, and the contract was transferred to them.

Beginning at Navy Bay and cutting through a deep morass and an almost impenetrable jungle recking with malaria the first fourteen miles of the line were laid, then by steep hillsides and over yawning chasms to the summit ridge, when it descended abruptly to the shores of the Pacific. Nor were these the only difficulties with which the engineers had to contend; for in consequence of the incompetency of the natives—a mixed race of Indians, Spaniards, and Negroes—labourers had to be imported, the resources of the country did not suffice for their support, and the Isthmian timber was not sufficiently durable for the work. All these were therefore brought from distant lands at great expense, while the sufferings of the workmen from fever, drenching rains, mosquitoes, sand-flies, and other insects fill the mind with horror when the details are described by those who witnessed or experienced them.

In May 1850 Mr Trautwine, with Mr Baldwin as assistant engineer, began the work of clearing where Colon now stands. But a residence on shore was soon declared impossible on account of the pestilential vapours, insufferable heat, reptiles of every description, and annoying insects, from whose maddening attacks

the gauze veils worn afforded little real
defence. In this emergency a brig was
hired, and into it the men repaired at
night; but even here their winged foes
appeared and soon compelled them to
vacate the cabin for the deck, where
drenching night rains caused the death
of many.

Later on the *Telegraph*, a condemned
steamship, was purchased for a residence,
and as the work progressed, shanties
on piles above the swamps were raised.
A surgeon next arrived, hospitals were
built, and the men received more care
and food. Yet, from various causes,
their numbers still decreased, financial
losses came, and for a few weeks the line
remained *in statu quo.* Then fresh
recruits were drafted in, and in October
1851 some working cars were drawn by

locomotive power to Gatun. This was followed by the transportation of passengers, who journeyed up the Chagres river by boat from the point where the railroad ceased, and then floundered through morasses and climbed the heights on mule-back until Panamá was reached—a mode of transit somewhat similar to Balboa's in 1513, I should say. But again financial difficulties and a scarcity of workmen barred the way, and almost a year elapsed before the company could resume the line at Barbacoas with the help of 7000 fresh hands. Many hundreds of these soon failed them, it is true, but the railroad was pushed on, and in January 1854 the summit range was reached. Only eleven miles now intervened between them and Panamá, where a movement to open a line and meet their friends was started; and on January 27, 1855, the grand object of running a locomotive from the Atlantic to the Pacific was attained, although many improvements had still to be made; and it was not until January 1859 that the railroad with sidings was complete; the cost up to that time having been 8,000,000 dollars, and the earnings 8,146,605 dollars.

Communication by land between the two oceans being now established, the next projected plan was to connect them by water also. But here, again, innumerable difficulties stopped its course; and the ill-fated Panamá Canal, engineered by the De Lesseps, begun in 1876, and abandoned in 1889, is still too fresh in public memory to need much comment. Great depression prevailed on the Isthmus

during our first visit there on account
of its abandonment, which proved a
crushing blow to shareholders. For a
considerable distance it accompanies the
railroad, and at La Boca, the Panamá
entrance, a number of vessels lie rotting,
while from different portions of the line
dredges and trucks are seen, all apparently useless, or regarded as such. Many
millions of francs are still required for
the completion of the work, and mean-
while the Nicaragua Canal is being rapidly
pushed forward by the States.

On leaving Colon by railroad, the
swampiness of the surrounding land first
strikes the traveller's gaze I think, and
then the curiously constructed wood or
bamboo huts raised on stone or wooden
piles above the swamps, and roofed with
palm leaves. Luxuriant vegetation lies

around, and the low mangrove bush with banyan-like propensities, the waving bamboo, and the many kinds of palm supplying sugar, sago, oil, flax, cocoa, and an endless list of articles of food and household vessels, excite his keenest wonder and delight. The giant cedro tree, mahogany, the *lignum vitæ*, and other valuable woods are found near Ahorca Lagarto too, and the sugar cane, maize, rice, the plantain, and banana wherever the ground is dry enough for cultivation.

Flowers during the dry season are both profuse and beautiful, and near Lion Hill the *peristera elata* orchid grows. Like the tulip in form, and sweetly scented, its blossoms are of snowy whiteness, and within the petals lies the image of a dove, hence its name *flor del Espiritu Santo*, flower of the Holy Ghost.

c

Many other orchids, the sensitive plant with pink, feathery blossoms and shrinking foliage, a great variety of the convolvulus creeper covering whole trees with clinging tendrils, aquatic plants, and parasites thrive well on the Isthmus too, whilst tropical fruits are represented by the bread-fruit, orange, lime, lemon, chirimoya or custard apple, mamei, palta, or alligator pear, pine apple, mango, and granadilla or passion fruit.

But less desirable and more alarming things live also in these marshy lands, and the boa-constrictor, alligator, scorpion, tarantula, and centipede are often seen, while the wild hog, ant-eater, tiger-cat, sloth, opossum, and monkey haunt the jungle close at hand.

The native population, including Spaniards, Indians, Negroes, and Half-castes, equip themselves with long, aggressive looking knives called *machetas*, and, I doubt not, know how to make good use of them when the occasion arises; but towards the stranger they display a kind and friendly air, and on the arrival of the trains appear to rouse themselves from a normal lethargic condition and take the keenest interest in the passers through. In the matter of clothing they are not extravagant, one or two thin garments sufficing for a full-grown representative of either sex, and the little children dispensing even with these, and running about in a nude condition. The ubiquitous Chinaman is here, of course, and at the different railway stations may generally be seen disposing of his wares and enjoying a pipe of peace, filled with opium.

Of the feathered tribe I may mention the gorgeous toucan, the oriole, or hanging bird, so called because it hangs its nest from the branches of trees, the parrot, parrakeet, wild turkey, pelican, grouse, heron, snipe, and humming bird. As elsewhere in the Tropics, songsters are rare, and the birds, as though in compensation, are dressed in brilliant plumage.

At Barbacoas a wrought-iron bridge, 625 feet in length, 18 in breadth, and 40 in height, spans the Chagres River, and is said to be one of the longest and finest bridges of its kind in the world. Still nearer to the summit, basaltic cliffs with an angle of forty degrees bespeak another instance of the natural perpendicular of these rocks having been displaced by some volcanic agency, and remind us of the Giant's Causeway and Fingal's Cave.

But the Cathedral towers of Panamá are looming in the distance, and at the terminus our minor packages are seized upon by hordes of youthful blacks, all striving to upset our equilibrium of mind as well as body. At length the medicine chests and all are saved, and borne away in carts, whilst we ensconce ourselves most gingerly in a dilapidated two-wheeled coach called buggy, and *hope* to reach the Grand Central Hotel ere nightfall, despite all shocks occasioned by the ruts and cobbled streets.

CHAPTER II.

THE city of Panamá has many historical associations, and its time-worn fortifications are full of interest for the antiquarian. Pizarro and his motley crew start into life before us now, and in the old Cathedral close at hand we almost see a crowd invoking Heaven's blessing on the Spanish arms about to seek a southern El Dorado, or we witness that strange contract for the disposition of an empire, not yet found, between Pizarro, Luque, and Almagro more than 360 years ago.

But modern Panamá stands on a peninsula six miles north-west of the ancient town destroyed by Henry Mor-

22

gan in 1661, and the knowledge that some other sacred building was the conquerors' resort reclaims our wandering thoughts.

The Republic of Colombia now includes New Granada, and with it Panamá, and Bogotá far inland is the capital. Many beautiful islands—notably those called Pearl Islands—adorn the spacious bay, and are much resorted to by invalids and others needing change from Panamá's malarial clime, while one of the most beautiful is known as Dead Man's Island, and appears to have been used as a sailors' burial ground in former days. Three other crowded cemeteries may now be seen when driving from the city to La Boca, and sadly warn us of the " great proprietor of all."

Like other South American towns,

Panamá boasts of an imposing-looking square or *plaza*, bordered by some of the principal buildings of the place, and ornamented in the centre with an array of shrubs and flowers. Facing the Grand Central Hotel and the Pacific Steam Navigation Company's Office, the Cathedral rears its head, while the remaining sides are occupied by the Archbishop's Palace, the Office of the *Compagnie Universelle du Canal Interocéanique*, and other public and private abodes. A Chinese store, with curios many and dear, is near the *plaza* too, and is well supported by passers through the city. Nevertheless, the Panamá attractions are not sufficient to compensate those who are compelled to spend a week there, and who require even a moderate amount of sleep and rest; for in the hotels mosqui-

toes and fleas dispute one's right to a
bed, and huge, brown cockroaches, and
strange-looking scorpions, monopolise the
boards free of rent during the—no, not
silent, for an incessant roll of coaches
over cobbled streets belies the adjective
—stirring watches of the night, while a
lighted candle, which scares the cock-
roach, only attracts the stinging gnat
through windows innocent of glass, and
furnished with Venetian blinds alone.
Robert Bruce could not have been personally acquainted with the mosquito, or
he would never have held up a spider as
the truest type of steady perseverance
I am sure: my own experience proves
that one mosquito would eclipse a whole
battalion of house spiders in tenacity of
purpose and design. One instance will
suffice. The wearied frame is sinking

into balmy sleep, and the brain at last forgets life's thousand ills, when forthwith comes a well-known *whizz*, which rouses every sinful passion into play, and then a fruitless chase takes place, only to be renewed at intervals the whole night through, until at dawn of day a brief and unrefreshing doze is snatched.

If we only could persuade the good old lady who looks after us that there *are* mosquitoes in the house, all might be well; but she (like the mosquitoes) is perverse, and feigning not to see the bites, still gives us tattered nets, which all our hairpins don't suffice to mend. The natives like a noise, but, strictly speaking, are not musical, if I may judge by the strange sounds that nightly emanated from their bands.

But the longest week must have an end, and, alas! for our ingratitude, the many kindnesses received from English and Colombian residents did not stop our hailing with delight a steamer for the south.

Two lines of steamers, the Pacific Steam Navigation and the Chilian, now ply between this port and Valparaiso, and two palatial boats have lately been added to each line, although the rival companies have recently amalgamated to some extent. Both are for the most part commanded by Englishmen and Americans; and here I would remark that the captains on the South Pacific coast consult the comfort and the welfare of the passengers most thoroughly, and are moreover courteous gentlemen to boot. The steamers, too, are good, and greatly we rejoiced in having deck cabins and square windows after frizzling down below in the West Indies with only tiny port-holes to afford a breath of air.

Embarking, then, on one of the P.S.N. Co's. vessels, we bade farewell to Panamá, and soon were sailing on a calm and peaceful ocean towards Callao.

The passengers were few, at least the loungers on the deck were so, for South Americans prefer the cabin's stifling heat, and are seldom seen from the time they embark until they go ashore again, but our cheery captain well supplied deficiencies, and a merry time was passed. Much more exciting, too, the voyage proved than that on the Atlantic side. Now, two days out of Panamá we reach the coast of Ecuador, pass San Lorenzo and the

line, and on the following day ran close
to Puná Island, where Pizarro in former
days defeated the natives and handed
them over to their enemies of Tumbez
on the mainland, while San Miguel, the
earliest Spanish settlement, lay in the
Tangarala valley not far off. The Gulf
of Guayaquil has many towns and
villages, behind which rise the dome-like
Chimborazo and volcanic Cotopaxi; and as
we gently sail upon the river, broad and
picturesque, the feathery-looking trees,
which skirt the neighbouring banks and
overhang the water's edge, entrance our
wondering gaze, while little rafts or
balsas darting in and out remind us of
the Indian craft described by Prescott.
Here oysters literally *grow on trees*, for
the low growing trees and bushes steep
their branches in the stream, and clinging

to them oysters are sometimes found.
But Nature, as though afraid of granting
all her choicest gifts upon one favoured
spot, has stocked these swampy banks
with alligators too !

Guayaquil is one of the largest towns
on the coast, and in former days her
dockyards were important. Hammocks,
and the celebrated Panamá hats made
from the leaves of the *bombandje* plaited
under water, are manufactured here, and
bananas and other fruits, quinine, sarsa-
parilla, and some silver are among her
many exports. We did not go ashore
here now, but on my return journey I
was enabled, through the kindness of a
fellow-passenger, to obtain a fuller knowledge of the place, and was introduced
to the ex-President, who in turn handed
us over to the captain of the port to be

conveyed back to the steamer in his six-oared boat.

The Andes traverse Ecuador from north to south, and Quito, the capital, stands at an elevation of 9453 feet above the sea, and is about 150 miles from Guayaquil. Two Inca roads ran formerly from Atahualpa's capital to Cuzco, 1500 miles, one being cut through a mountainous country, and the other along the maritime plain for a considerable distance.

The famous Emerald mine from which the Incas enriched their treasury was in the neighbourhood of Quito too; and when at Guayaquil we thought of Gallo, where those thirteen heroes crossed the line Pizarro drew upon the sand, and dared to share with him the hardships of his " trial trip."

The town of Piura, celebrated for its
fine breed of mules, lies in the interior,
and is connected with Guayaquil by railroad.   On leaving this port a change in
the character ·of the coast line appeared,
and henceforth sandy treeless strips
supplied the place of verdure.

At Paita we anchored and shipped some
cattle ; but the brutal way in which they
were hoisted, by means of ropes round
the horns, from barges into the steamer,
upon the deck of which they generally
fell struggling or stunned, aroused my
deepest indignation and disgust.   Paita,
on account of its freedom from mists
and clouds, is said to be admirably
adapted for an astronomical observatory,
as the stars are nearly always visible at
night, and shine with greater brilliancy
than elsewhere.   It may be so, but I

should greatly pity the astronomers located there with nothing but a sandy waste around. "As bright as the moon at Paita," is an old and well-known simile. Trujillo, founded by Pizarro, and named in honour of his birthplace, joins this port by rail, and is a thriving and important business place.

Pacasmayo was next passed, and at the port of Salaverry the shipping and unloading detained us for some hours. Then all was bustle in our floating house, excitement reigned supreme, and vain attempts were made to stow away vast purchases in spaces inelastic, as in the deepening twilight we watched our friend's approach in Callao Bay, and knew that we had reached our present destination.

The ancient town of Callao was entirely destroyed by earthquake in 1746, and

D

Lima partially so : both suffered in the Arica earthquake of 1828, and a tidal wave in 1868 caused an incalculable amount of damage and loss to life and property. Two lines of railroad connect the port with Lima, eight miles inland, and soon we find ourselves borne off in an American car to the Peruvian capital, built by Pizarro, and called by him *Ciudad de los Reyes*—City of the Kings—in honor of the Feast of the Epiphany (January 6, 1535), the day on which its site was determined. Later on the city was called Rimac from the oracle, and finally became converted into Lima.

Peru was a name given to the country by its Spanish conquerors, but the origin of the word is buried in obscurity, and many and curious are the derivations given. Pascual de Andagoya traces it to

the province of Birú, Father Valera to the
Quichua word Pirua, a granary, and the
imaginative Garcillasso de la Vega to the
ancient Ophir,—ever open to location.
The Incas called their country Tavantin-
suyu—four quarters of the world—and
intersected it with four great roads
emanating from Cuzco.

Modern Peruvians think the country
was named from Viru, an Indian district
near Trujillo.

CHAPTER III.

EVEN in the abstract, war and desolation are much to be deplored; but when we see a beautifully embellished city laid low by the hand of wanton destruction, our inmost nature groans. Such is Lima of the present day; and although eight years have passed away since that disastrous Chilian war, she still bears traces of the ravages committed then, and her many roofless and dismantled houses awaken sentiments of pity and regret.

Yet she has somewhat recovered from that crushing blow, and the wonted light-heartedness of the Peruvian returns as he sees the nation's commerce improve, and his own finances with it.

Strange as it may seem, guano and nitrates—two sources of wealth—have proved as fatal to the modern Peruvian as gold and silver were of yore; for were not these deposits the true and direct cause of the Chilian invasion and its deplorable results? Her ironclads were taken or destroyed, the guano and saltpetre provinces of Tacna and Tarapaca possessed by the enemy, and a prosperous country pillaged and left a ruin. What the result of the *plebiscitum* in 1893 may be, when a final settlement of the provinces handed over to Chili by the peace of Ancon in 1883 takes place, who can tell?

But to return to the present condition of Lima. In the *plaza mayor*, about 500 feet square, stand some of the most important buildings in the city. The

President's Palace and Government offices are on its north side, and the imposing looking Cathedral approached by a broad expanse of steps, and containing solid silver pillars and a quantity of silver plate, is on the east, where also the Archbishop's residence is found. The remaining sides contain attractive looking shops under *portales*, over which the *Municipalidad* and gentlemen's clubs are seen, all having spacious balconies, densely crowded with spectators on the occasion of a public rejoicing in the square. In the *Callejon de Petateros* (matmakers' alley), an outlet from the square, Pizarro's house once stood, and here it was that he was killed by young Almagro's followers. His remains now repose in the new Cathedral beside those of the good Viceroy Mendoza, and visitors still solicit portions of his cloak, which has been renewed on several occasions since the conqueror's death to meet the general demand! From the two towers of the Cathedral the bodies of two of the notorious Gutierrez brothers were suspended after the murder of President Balta in 1872; they were then taken down and publicly burned in the square.

Flower beds and ornamental shrubs adorn the middle of the *plaza*, where also a fountain surmounted by a bronze figure of Fame, erected by Count de Salvatierra, Spanish Viceroy in 1653, and many colossal statues are placed, while the longitudinal streets debouching therefrom are arranged in blocks and traversed by tramcars. "*Calle de la Mercaderes*" (the merchants' street), to the south of the *plaza*, is the best for shops. Here jewellers, modistes, drapers, and silversmiths display their precious goods, and here the beauty and youth of Lima resort from four to six o'clock. In various parts of the city some handsome bridges span the river Rimac, notably that of Desamparados, where fruit and other vendors ensconce themselves in niches and sell their wares to passers-by.

Earthquakes are frequent here, but many of the houses are two and even three stories high, and the flat Oriental roofs are used for drying grounds and other purposes. An entrance gateway forms the approach to many of the private residences, which is carefully locked during revolutionary tumults. In these houses the dwelling rooms are round a square, with the centre space,

or *patio*, open to the sky, and all the
lower windows are closely barred with
iron rods. Balconies or *miradores* form
a pleasant outlook from most of the
houses, and wood-carving often relieves
them. The mansion of the Marquis of
Torre Tagle, built of stone, and richly
ornamented with wood-carving, is especially worthy of note.

Imported fruits abound, and residents
frequent the market at an early hour to
purchase fruit and flowers. The large
Chinese quarter lies in the same neighbourhood too, and not far off the National
Library is found, and well deserves a
look, although the Chilians have robbed
it of many valuable collections of paint-
ings and of books. Montero's grand
picture of "The Funeral Obsequies of
Atahualpa, the Last of the Incas," is

there, and graphically depicts the
touching ceremony. His body lies in
state enveloped in a scarlet robe, and as
the friar Valverde gabbles through the
service for the dead, Pizarro and his
cavaliers stand grouped around. But
presently loud cries are heard without,
and suddenly some Indians, the wives
and near relatives of the murdered man,
rush wildly up the aisle and press around
the corpse, exclaiming, "This is not the
way to perform an Inca's funeral rites."
They then propose to sacrifice themselves
upon his tomb and go with him to the
region of the Sun. Such conduct horrifies
the Spaniards, and after explaining
that Atahualpa had died in the faith
of a Christian, they thrust the intruders
from the sacred edifice. Silenced, but not
convinced, the unhappy women retire to

their abodes, where many lay violent hands upon themselves in the hope of following their beloved lord to the sunny land whither he was gone.

Pizarro's portrait too is seen with those of the other viceroys in the National Library of Lima; and, as this remarkable man has played so conspicuous a part in Peruvian history, I purpose giving a brief outline of his career.

The illegitimate child of Gonzalo Pizarro, a colonel of infantry, and Francisca Gonzales, a woman of humble origin, and born probably about the year 1471, Francisco's chief occupation in early life seems to have been that of a swineherd, which so little suited his adventurous spirit that he escaped from his native place Truxillo, in Estremadura, to Seville, and there joined his enterprising countrymen in seeking a fortune in the New World. His education had been entirely neglected, and to the time of his death his signature was attested by a *rúbrica* or flourish. After serving in Hispaniola, and accompanying Balboa in his terrible march across the Isthmus of Panamá, he was appointed to succeed Andagoya in commanding an expedition having for its object the discovery and conquest of a southern El Dorado.

Innumerable perils and hardships tracked his course, but the great Peruvian empire was at length added to the Spanish crown ; and Charles V., in recognition of his services, and after much delay, enriched him with absolute authority in the conquered land and the title of *Marques de la Conquista*. The foul murder of the last great Inca did not, however, entail a peaceable possession; and, as might have been expected from the lawless and avaricious nature of the conquerors, they soon disputed amongst themselves, until at length the Marquis himself was murdered by his countrymen in his own house.

In reviewing the character of Pizarro, our judgment must necessarily be guided, to a very great extent, by his early life and the lawless nature of those amongst whom his lot was cast. That avarice and ambition ruled his actions we can have no doubt, and treachery and cruelty most sadly marked his course. Nevertheless, we distinguish in him a courageous and inflexible constancy that constituted the secret of his great success, and his followers saw in him a leader who felt for them as one soldier for another, and

never hesitated to share their greatest
toils.

Almost irreligious himself, he yet proclaimed the message of the Cross—for the
early conquerors were deeply imbued with
the *theory* of religion, however much their
own conduct may have belied the *practice!*
—and by his hardships and endurance
enriched the crown of Spain with one of
her richest jewels. Tall, well-proportioned,
and not unpleasing in appearance, he was
unostentatious in dress, and wore on public
occasions a black cloak and white hat,
while his portrait now on view depicts
him in a citizen's dress and black hat.

Southey's lines on the Conqueror do
not flatter him, but they may not be
considered an inapt summary of his
career. They were designed for a column
at Truxillo—

" Pizarro here was born ; a greater name
    The list of Glory boasts not.   Toil and Pain,
    Famine, and hostile Elements, and Hosts embattled
    Failed to check him in his course.
    Not to be wearied, not to be deterred,
    Not to be overcome.   A mighty realm
    He overran, and with relentless arm
    Slew or enslaved its unoffending sons,
    And wealth and power and fame were his rewards.
    There is another world, beyond the grave,
    According to their deeds where men are judged.
    O Reader, if thy daily bread be earned
    By daily labour ; yea, however low.
    However wretched, be thy lot assigned,
    Thank thou, with deepest gratitude, the God
    Who made thee, that thou art not such as he."

Lima boasts of many hotels, but for families the most desirable are the " Maury " and the " Hotel de Francia y Inglaterra." Should your Spanish be deficient, French is perfectly understood in both.

The milkwoman, a Chola or negress seated on a mule between her cans, and wearing a Panamá straw hat, and the waterman on mule or donkey with his jars, are common sights in all the streets, where also on two or three days of the week men selling lottery tickets are frequently seen.

El Comercio, *El Constitucional*, *El Nacional*, and *El Pais* are the leading newspapers of Peru, and represent in some form or other the politics of the nation.

Roman Catholicism prevails, and Lima is essentially a city of churches, monasteries, and convents. Of churches there are said to be more than sixty, many of them having finely carved façades.

Santo Domingo is the oldest, and San Francisco near the Rimac, and San

Pedro with its grand oak altars may be
mentioned as the finest. The two high
towers of San Francisco have stood
some sharp attacks, and bear more bullet
holes than the cathedral front. To the
Madonna within the niche in the *Capella
del Milagro* legend ascribes the safety
of the city during the great earthquake
of November 1630. Her effigy, it is
said, was placed over the porch facing
the street ; but whilst earnestly praying
for the city's preservation during the
shock, she changed her position, and
was afterwards discovered facing the high
altar ! La Merced in the Mercaderes is
much frequented by worshippers too, and
has an exquisitely carved façade. But
all the churches, even the cathedral, are
poorly built, and consist for the most
part of cane, timber, and sun-dried bricks

E

faced with stucco ; the same may be said
of most of the houses. Saint days are
general holidays, and after Mass is over
the city is *en fête*.

Santa Rosa de Santa Maria is the
patron saint of Lima, and on August
30th her effigy is borne about the streets
and into various churches.   Unlike the
rest of humanity, this good woman was
not afflicted with sufficient bodily pain
to suit her pious nature, and with a
determination worthy of a better cause,
encircled her waist with an iron belt in
penance for her sins.   Fearing that physical torture would induce her to free
herself from its unwelcome grasp, she
boldly locked the belt, and nipped a sore
temptation in the bud by dropping the
key into an apparently bottomless well,
which is still pointed out as the recep-

tacle of the voluntary gift! I looked down into it, but saw nothing of the key! It never seems to have occurred to the girl or her friends that a locksmith might solve the difficulty, and she lived and died a saint! Religious practices are strictly observed by the Limeñas, who throng the streets at an early hour on their way to and from the different churches. The devotion of the men is not so noticeable.

In honour of Peruvian emancipation from Spain on July 28th, 1821, after an occupation of nearly 300 years, the 28th, 29th, and 30th of July are national holidays, and a general rejoicing takes place. Business houses and shops are closed for those three days, flags of all nationalities adorn the streets, services are held in the cathedral and other churches, bands of music and processions, both military and religious, parade the city, and as night advances balls are held and fireworks let off. To us it seemed quite natural to come in for Republican rejoicings again, as we had swelled the strains of Yankee Doodle on the American day at St Thomas, and had been in time for the Marseillaise and illuminations at Panamá.

Peruvian ladies, and females of all classes, wear *mantas* of a crape-like material, which conceal almost the whole person, and answer the double purpose of bonnet and shawl, for church and morning shopping, but the European style of dress for visiting and promenades. In summer weather a lace *mantilla* is often substituted for the heavier *manta*, and the graceful arrangement of both affords

much scope for the taste of the wearer.
It is considered highly improper for a
Limeña, either married or single, to walk
the streets alone, and the husband, a
lady friend, or a female servant, even
though she may be only fourteen or
fifteen years of age, is always discovered
in her train. How terribly imprudent,
then, must the independent foreigner
appear to their punctilious eyes! And
how they must have censured my lonely
reconnoitring strolls! But foreigners
lack that world-famed reputation for
beauty and grace that characterizes
Limeñas, and are moreover less accustomed to *surveillance*. About the middle
height, Limeñas have pale, dark, clear
complexions, greatly aided by cosme-
tics, bright black eyes and glossy hair,
tiny feet, exquisite teeth, a vivacious,

pleasing style, and are most graceful dancers. Young ladies are, as a rule, slight in figure, but the married and elderly are decidedly inclined to fleshiness, which is not to be wondered at, seeing they take so little walking exercise, and often engage a coach to convey them from one street into the next.

Now the Lima coach is a special study, for it takes two horses to draw it in its (generally) dilapidated condition over the cobbles, and they are so poor that I have known them stop altogether, and the driver transfer his passengers into another vehicle. The enervating climate has doubtless a great deal to do with their enfeebled condition, and the coachman lends a helping hand, for his whip is seldom at rest.

Love of gaiety is a national feature,

and the theatres are densely crowded when anything really good is on; for the Peruvians are a musical people, and the light Italian operatic style is more pleasing to their ears than solid German strains, although the best German composers are greatly appreciated too. Ladies dress superbly for the play; and their bright costumes, diamonds, and glittering gems make the opera house a striking picture. This is a favourite time for visiting too, and between the acts it is customary for gentlemen to call upon their lady friends in the boxes.

Ceremonious visits are usually made in the afternoon, as with us, but gentlemen who have little leisure during these hours call in the evening after dinner.

I may be wrong, but, taken as a whole,

it struck me that the Peruanas are superior to the men, both morally and in intellectual attainments, although individually it was my privilege to know some noble members of the sterner sex. They are usually about the middle height, and remind one of an European Spaniard.

Bull-baiting formerly attracted crowds of Limeñas to the Plaza de Accho, but this barbarous sport is now encouraged by the men alone. Gambling is still a favourite pastime, and reminded me of an incident connected with one of the early conquerors who received, as his share of the spoil, an image of the sun raised on a plate of burnished gold, and torn from the walls of the temple of Cuzco. This plate he gambled away one night, and thus gave rise to the Spanish proverb, "*Juego el Sol antes que amanezca*"—He· plays away the sun before sunrise.

A large cemetery on the outskirts of Lima is well kept, and contains some handsome monuments ; while the Exhibition and Botanic Gardens, and the *Alameda de Descalzos*, form delightful promenades, gay with exquisite roses and flowers of every shade and hue. But here, as elsewhere, the total absence of grass detracts considerably from the beauty of the flowers, and the dry parched look on every side is very trying to an English eye.

CHAPTER IV.

No heavy rain falls on this portion of
the Pacific coast, and clouds of sand and
dust are ever in the air. December and
January are generally the warmest months
in the year, and the maximum summer
heat is 78° Fahrenheit, and the winter
60° or thereabout. The Humboldt
current from the Antarctic causes the
temperature to be lower here than in the
same latitude on the Brazilian coast, and
for this reason the Peruvian climate is
healthier, although at times a great
amount of malarial fever (terceanus)
prevails, and particularly during the
winter months, when a thick mist arises

with the approach of night and penetrates the airy houses. Fireplaces in sitting rooms and bedrooms are unknown, although a little artificial heat at these times would be most acceptable.

Of late years no great damage has been done by earthquakes, and the first we felt, soon after our arrival, was the worst that has been known in Lima for a long time. Indeed, I was not anxious for a severer shock, as this one drove me from my bedroom on the third floor to the corridor of the hotel at six A.M. The house seemed wrapped in sleep; and remembering that I was but slightly clad, I hastily withdrew again to wait in terror for another shock, which fortunately never came, and soon the great Cathedral bell proclaimed the city's thankfulness for dangers past. Later in the day we learned that on account of the shock being so prolonged and strong it was greatly feared many high and ancient buildings would have given way, but happily no harm was done.

The English church is a good-sized, comfortable building, and the services attractive and well conducted, but Church-going Protestants are in a sad minority.

Holy Week is observed with great solemnity by Peruvians generally, and at mid-day on the Thursday all trains and coaches cease running, and no whistling of engines nor ringing of bells is permitted at the railway stations. Private pianos and other musical instruments remain untouched, and the inhabitants of Lima clothe themselves in black for the occasion. On this day good Romanists

are expected to attend seven of the
church's services, where and when they
please, and the sacred buildings with
draperies and flowers present a gorgeous
look, particularly during the evening
illuminations. In some of them nuns,
who are seen by the outside world on
this night *only* during the year, chant
services behind the wooden bars; and
until recently the Last Supper and the
"rending of the vail" took place in Santo
Domingo or some other church. The abuse
of the former by the priests led to its
abolition. At nine A.M. on Saturday all
mourning ceases, for Peruvians forestall
events, and the return to activity and
bustle is begun by the pealing of church
bells.

Hats and bonnets are strictly pro-
hibited in all the churches at all times;

and however careful the stranger may be in conforming to established rules, he or she is soon detected by some watchful eye. I remember visiting the Cathedral one morning soon after our arrival and finding a priest attended by two acolytes standing at the altar, and murmuring some prayers. Anxious not to disturb the worshippers, we quietly crept down the side aisle, and were engaged in examining the pillars, when one of the acolytes, whom we imagined too devoutly praying to notice our entrance, touched us on the arms and begged for alms.

Lima supports many hospitals, chiefly by the sale of lottery tickets; and at the Franciscan Monastery of Descalzos much charitable work is done by the friars, who wear a long, coarse, greyish coat with hood, and sandals. Daily, at a certain hour, food is dispensed to the needy at a postern gate, and the charities and good offices of the friars extend far into the interior of Peru as well. They usually travel in couples, an old and a young one together, and rarely leave the monastery except on missions of mercy.

On the Sunday, Monday, and Tuesday before Lent a Carnival is observed in Lima, when all who are bold enough to walk the streets must expect to be deluged with water from the balconies above. *Chisgetes*, or scent-squirts, too, are freely used by those who play; and when the wretched victim has been soaked with these, tiny coloured squares of paper mixed with powder are thrown upon the hair, and cause an infinite amount of pains to extricate.

The watering-places of Miraflores, Barranco, and Chorrillos are all connected with the capital by rail, and possess some good and picturesque-looking *ranchos*. Here many of the business people of Lima have private residences, and previous to the war they were doubtless gay and thickly populated suburbs, but now, more or less, show signs of the enemy's desolating course.

Around these three villages the chief incidents of the war with Chili took place. At 5 A.M., on that memorable 13th of January 1881, firing commenced around the Morro Solar defence, and at 2 P.M. Chorrillos was in flames, foreign and neutral flags torn down, the British Minister's house, the church and other public buildings, levelled with the ground, and the Military College converted into a hospital for the wounded conquerors.

VERRUGAS BRIDGE.

Barranco suffered almost as much, and at 2.45 P.M. on the 16th, fighting commenced near Miraflores, and was continued with unabated fury until 6.45 P.M., when this village also was in flames, and an overwhelming number of soldiers, merchants, students, and mechanics lay dead around the defence, and amidst the ruined houses. In the two engagements 6000 Peruvians are said to have been killed, and 3000 wounded, while the Chilian loss is estimated at 1300 killed and 4144 wounded.

Lima would have suffered the same sad fate as Chorrillos and Miraflores had it not been for the stout resistance made by the English Minister, Sir Spencer St. John, and the material aid afforded by the English and French Admirals; while it was due to the united efforts of the foreign

F

volunteers that the city was not sacked
on the night of that disastrous 16th.
On the following day it was formally
surrendered by the municipal *Alcalde*,
and General Baquedano established himself in the Palace, but a Provisional
Government was afterwards formed under
Francisco Garcia Calderon, a lawyer of
Arequipa.

It surely is a matter of congratulation
to us, as a nation, that some of our own
countrymen have been instrumental in
freeing Peru from her oppressors.   Her
freedom from Spain was to a great extent
due to the exertions of Admiral Cochrane
(Lord Dundonald) and his gallant English
officers; and during the late war with
Chili, the English, American, and other
foreign residents were eminently distinguished for their ready help in fighting

the invaders. Some of the most important business houses, too, are in the hands
of Englishmen and Americans, and the
export trade, which is extensive, is prin-
cipally with England.

Owing to the lack of moisture, few
things grow well near the coast, but in
the occasional fertile valleys the sugar
cane and cotton plant abound. Agricul-
ture is, however, in a backward state, and
oxen are still used to draw the plough;
but the manufacture of *ponchos* (rugs
having a hole in the centre for the head
to go through, and much worn by
dwellers in the mountains and others),
blankets, mats, and *bufandas* (vicuña
shawls), as well as exquisite filigree work,
employs large numbers in the interior.
The mining resources are extensive, and
Peru exports bar silver, copper, tin, lead,

some gold, guano, nitrates of soda and borax, wool, sugar, alpaca, cotton, hides, Peruvian bark, coca, etc.

Statistics are tedious, and shall be avoided, but the value of the guano and saltpetre deposits may be gathered from the fact that in 1875 Peru exported to foreign countries 378,687 tons of guano, and in 1878 269,327 tons of nitrate of soda left the ports of Tarapaca. What wonder that the Chilians coveted the provinces possessing both! They are found where no rain falls; and as every drop of moisture is extracted from the Atlantic winds when they reach the snowy summit of the Andes, the dry Pacific coast is well suited for both deposits.

The word "guano" takes its name from the *huana*, immense flocks of

which frequent the Chincha and Guanapa
Islands and the coast of Tarapaca, and
produce the valuable manure. They are
sea-birds with black plumage, and about
the size of gulls. Each nest contains a
fledged bird, an unfledged one, and an
egg, and they breed throughout the year.

The discovery by the Spaniards of the
invaluable cinchona or Peruvian bark
was accidental and remarkable. Tradition
says that when one of the early conquerors fell sick with fever (terceanus),
an Indian girl in love with him was
discovered mixing a powder with his
medicine. As she persistently refused
to reveal its virtues, the Spaniards
thought that she sought to poison their
countryman, and threatened her with
torture, whereupon she confessed to the
bark's curative properties, and inadvert-

ently conferred a lasting boon upon humanity at large in this new febrifuge.

Both Peru and Bolivia export large quantities of "the bark of barks," and plantations of it are found as high as 6000 feet above the sea. The tree, which belongs to the same order as the coffee plant, resembles the beech in general appearance, and its white wood is capable of being highly polished. Over 3,000,000 pounds of bark are shipped annually to England alone, and each tree at six years of age yields from five to six pounds.

An abundance of tropical fruit stocks the Lima market and the stalls of itinerant vendors, such as the delicious chirimoya, the granadilla or passion fruit, pine apple, banana, fig, quince, pomegranate, guava, palta, tuna, or cactus fruit, orange, lime, lemon, peach, etc., but most of it comes from the interior or from Guayaquil. The yellow, sweet, and a variety of other potatoes, the yucca, Indian corn, and beans grow near the coast, and are largely consumed.

Most of the native dishes are tasty and *picante*; and amongst them I may name a soup called *chupe*, made by boiling fish, cheese, eggs, and potatoes together, and *seviche*, fish cooked in lemon or sour orange juice, and strongly flavoured with *aji* (pepper). *Cancha*, or Indian corn roasted, is generally eaten with this dish, and *chicha* accompanies it. This beverage, usually made with maize, somewhat resembles cider in taste, and seems to have been a royal luxury in the days of Atahualpa; for we read that when Hernando Pizarro and De Soto visited the monarch, they gratefully quaffed the chicha presented to them by the bewitching beauties of the harem. *Olla podrida*, or *puchero*, is another favourite dish, and consists of meat mixed with sweet potato, almost any vegetables, rice and cassava root boiled together. Of *dulces* those under the generic name of *masamorra*, a sweet farinaceous mixture, compotes, and small pastries are most in favour.

Smoking is much indulged in by Peruvian men, and at the hotel dinner tables during coffee, in the trains, and almost everywhere they may be seen twirling their cigarettes; so that, in order to live with any degree of comfort in this land of smokers, one's strongest objections must be overcome.

The valley of Pisco and many other districts are noted for vineyards, and the spirit called *Italia*, and the wines of Moquegua and Ilo are much esteemed.

Neither gold coinage nor paper money has currency at the present day, and the clumsy silver *sol* possesses the highest value. It varies with the price of silver, from 2s. 9d. to 3s. 6d. of our money, and is rather larger than a half-crown piece. The *peseta* is a fifth of a *sol*, and a *cent* is the lowest coin. The depreciation of paper money, occasioned by the Chilian war, reduced many previously wealthy families to poverty, and notes that formerly represented large fortunes now became waste paper.

Lima with its population of 130,000 embraces Peruvians, Spaniards, Indians, Negroes, Half-castes, including Sambos, or one parent black and the other mulatto;

Chinos, one parent black and the other Indian; Mestisos, one parent white and the other Indian; and Mulattos, one parent white and the other negro, Italians, Frenchmen, Germans, Englishmen, Americans, and Chinamen; but all live in apparent unity, and the political riots at Presidential elections now form the greatest drawback to the country's peace and progress.

On the retirement of Don Andres Avelina Caceres in 1890, Dr Rosas, Don Nicholas de Piérola, and Colonel Remjio Morales Bermudez came forward as candidates for the office of President; a contest that resulted in the election of Colonel Bermudez in April and his installation a few months later.

Piérola had been proclaimed Supreme Chief of the Republic during the Chilian

war, and greatly distinguished himself
in the battles of Chorrillos and Miraflores ;
but some old charges were brought up
against him when he appeared as a
candidate for power in April 1890, and
he was moreover accused of introducing
insurrectionary troops into the city, which
led to his arrest by command of President Caceres and confinement in the
Intendencia until the election was over.
Great was my surprise on reaching Lima
from Barranco on Easter morning to
hear of Piérola's imprisonment. He
married a grand-daughter of Agustin
Iturbide, the unfortunate Emperor of
Mexico, and is described as pleasing in
appearance, and possessed of a clear
intellect, a vivacious manner, and great
tenacity of purpose.

Four years is the President's term of

office, and he cannot be re-elected until
the same number of years have elapsed.
In the Executive he is assisted by
a Vice-President and responsible min-
isters, and the Constitution itself is composed of three independent bodies—the
executive, legislative, and judicial corps.
All Peruvians have a vote, and *nominally*
the nation at large elects the President;
but *actually* the provincial deputies
name the electors, and these the President.

The nineteen departments are ruled by
prefects, and the provinces within them
by sub-prefects, all of whom are chosen
by the President. Complaints against the
Government are settled by the Supreme
Court of Justice, and an *Alcalde* or
Mayor elected by the public from in-
fluential classes controls all local affairs.

The total area of the country covers

500,000 square miles, and at the last census in 1876 the population was estimated at 2,970,000. The regular army now consists of 5000 men, and the navy exists in name alone. British interests in Peru are represented by Colonel Sir Charles Mansfield, K.C.M.G. (1890), and those of the United States by Mr Hicks.

The Lima policemen struck me as a class worthy of special notice. They are clothed somewhat like the soldiers, are seldom seen to interfere when a breach of the law takes place, and at every half hour during the night are obliged to blow a whistle to convince the public that they are awake, and may be found if wanted.

Amongst the scientific and remarkable men who have shed a lustre on the Peruvian nation, I would name Paz Soldan

and Antonia Raimondi, geographers;
Sebastian Lorente, historian; Ricardo
Palma, historian and novelist; Laso and
Montero, painters; Luis Medina, sculptor;
Melgar, Althaus, and Marquez, poets; and
Mariano Eduardo Rivero, mineralogist
and director-general of mines. Universi-
ties, state colleges for boys and girls,
military and naval institutions, and
schools of mines now exist in Peru,
and bespeak the nation's educational
desires.

II.

In the Sierra.

CHAPTER I.

SINCE the Chilian war, for all recent mundane Peruvian affairs seem to date from that catastrophe, the boundaries of the country may be said to extend from 1° to 19° S., and from 68° to 81° W., the river Camerones forming her southern boundary in accordance with the terms of the treaty of Ancon in 1883. Lima lies in the 12th parallel. The Republic is bounded on the north by Ecuador, on the south by Chili, on the east by the Brazils and Bolivia, and on the west by the Pacific Ocean; while the Andes, a continuation of the Rocky Mountains of North America, traverse it from N.E. to S.W., and divide the country into three distinct regions—the Coast, the Puna or Sierra, and the Montaña.

The arid coast line I have already noticed, and the montaña, or forest land, which includes that almost limitless, and to a great extent, undeveloped country watered by the Amazon and Ucayali rivers east of the Cordillera, where the cinchona and caucho or india rubber trees abound, and where cocoa, coffee, cotton, vanilla, coca, and tobacco more especially flourish, is somewhat too vast for my present purpose.

It is then of a portion of the Sierra or Central region, where fertile valleys occur, where precious metals are found, and where the gentle llama finds its home, that I will now particularly treat.

To quote the different ideas we entertained

LANDSCAPE, SHOWING CREST OF THE SOUTH AMERICAN CONTINENT, 24,000 FEET.

of this region before our ascent would
require a three-volumed work at least,
and the packing of our clothes, etc., in
sacks to be conveyed on mule-back was
as exciting as the many other preparations
for the trip. In this matter our chief
difficulty generally lay in finding out what
we should *not* require. At one time we
imagined ourselves arriving at the summit,
17,000 feet, tied on our mules, and in a
bruised and battered condition, occasioned
by numerous headlong journeys down the
precipices, only to die of "sorroche" and
cold; at another, the spirit of adventure
filled up the vacuum, and a sharp encoun-
ter with the Indians obliged us to flee
for our lives; or again, the delightful
sensation of being borne on the wings of
the wind, or the legs of the mules,
through sunshine and snow into Nature's

sanctorum itself, composed our restless
minds, and we revelled in the thought.

One thing seemed certain, and that
was that in the region whither we were
bound fleas could not live, which after
our late experience would be much
appreciated.

But our reception in the metropolis
had been as cordial as the most fastidious
could desire, and its many attractions
were hard to leave for so indefinite and
vague a trip; yet even these must be
forsaken for a while, as we wing our
upward flight.

Leaving the Desamparados station by
the great Oroya railroad early one morning in September, and having a mining
hacienda in the department of Junin,
and not far from the town of Yauli as
our destination, we threaded the valley

of the once sacred Rimac, and in a couple of hours arrived at the health-giving village of Chosica, 2832 feet above the waters of the Pacific. Here a halt was made, and for several weeks we scoured the country on horseback and on foot at will, often climbing such rocky staircases that no animals but *chuscos* and mules born and bred to the work would have attempted. The bright, sunshiny weather, more bracing climate, and glorious sunsets rejoice us greatly after Lima's wintry gloom ; but the bare and rocky heights around where only cacti flourish look dreary and forbidding, and the many *gallinasos* or turkey buzzards depress us with their melancholy look. These huge black birds are general scavengers, and in former days he who dared shoot one was subjected thereby to five soles' penalty. They are still treated with respect as inexpensive workmen, and are rarely destroyed.

Chosica is a favourite resort for those afflicted with pulmonary complaints, and our healthy appearance, good appetite, and general energy are quite abnormal here. Indeed, when the question arose as to which was the invalid of the party, our consciences sorely smote us for enjoying such perfect health when all around were sick. The principal hotel is at the station, and great is the excitement of its inmates when the bi-weekly trains arrive to and from the interior and Lima. A general rush is made from every part of the building, invalids revive, sleepers awake, and many and wonderful are the greetings and embraces exchanged, for in this friendly district everybody is the partic-

ular friend of everybody else. Embracing
and patting first one shoulder and then
the other is a great feature in Peruvian
greetings, both amongst men and women,
and it always surprised me that there
was no confusion of arms on these occasions. I tried it once or twice, but got
hopelessly entangled, and appeared to be
fighting through using the wrong arm
first! ·

On Sundays, too, a pleasure train leaves
Lima for Chosica, laden with passengers
eager to breathe the invigorating mountain
air, if only for a few short hours, and
returns the same evening.

During the enervating winter season
on the coast the hotel is generally well
patronised, and with walking, riding,
dancing, and cards, some pleasant days
may be spent here.

Many varieties of the cactus shrub bristle amongst the surrounding rocks, and in the valleys the banana, palta, and granadilla fruits, the castor-oil plant, acacia, wild pepper, datura, called *floripondio*, with large, white, bell-shaped blossoms and powerful scent especially at dusk, the cheerful looking broom, hibiscus, and blue-green eucalyptus flourish.

But our three weeks' sojourn is drawing to a close, and once more we seat ourselves in an American car on the Oroya line, and journey on to San Bartolomé, fifty miles from Lima, and 4949 feet above the ocean level. Here, funny little cane huts, llamas, and an abundance of tropical fruits dispensed by Indian men and women invite our curiosity, and here, too, our railroad

journey ends, owing to many parts of
the line further on having been washed
away by mountain floods in February
1889. But the foresight of our kind
and worthy escort has furnished us with
surefooted mountain mules — animals
similar to those described by Prescott
as having been created for the Cordillera
—for further transit, and on these we
scale the mountain paths to Verrugas
Bridge, where the heat is almost stifling.
But the steep ascent in one place obliged
us to dismount and crawl on hands and
feet, for which we were rewarded by
being able to pluck some exquisite
blossoms from the heliotrope trees
around. A disease called "verrugas,"
which appears in the form of immense
warts on the face and body, and occasions
much internal pain, prevails in this

locality, and is attributed by some authorities to the turning over of fresh soil, and by others to injurious properties in the water of the neighbourhood. Be that as it may, the disease is difficult to cure; and if not brought out of the system on to the surface of the body by perspiration, generally proves fatal. It may frequently be seen disfiguring the faces of the workmen here, and during the erection of the bridge as many as eighteen daily are said to have succumbed to it. Most passers through are careful in the matter of drinking water, and take only that which has been boiled.

Verrugas Bridge, composed of wrought-iron columns, is considered one of the greatest feats of engineering skill. It spans a chasm of 580 feet, and formerly

rested upon three piers at a height of
252 feet above the abyss. The centre
pier was, however, completely destroyed
by the February floods; and now (1890)
when the line is re-opened as far as
Chicla, passengers are conveyed from one
side of the bridge to the other in a
little open car, suspended by chains
over the yawning chasm. Phœnixville,
U.S.A., had the honour of engineering
the stupendous work, and its cost was
estimated at 63,000 dollars. But this
has recently been superseded by a new
bridge, which we met on our return
journey through Panama, and which
doubtless makes a pleasanter and more
convenient mode of transit than the
temporary car, which occasioned so much
delay while waiting for trains on either
side, to say nothing of the shock to one's

nerves during those thirty-seven seconds of suspension !

Still pursuing our novel expedition on mule-back, sometimes by the railroad track and through tunnels in the solid rock, past deserted Indian villages, magnificent cañons and waterfalls, the lonely peasant's hut clinging to the sides of the mountains, and remains of Inca terraced gardens; up steep and narrow paths beside the restless river, through the village of Surco, where we paused for tea, and on to Matucana as the fast approaching twilight sinks into blackest night. Most gladly did we here alight and take our evening meal ere balmy sleep refreshed our weary frames. The hotel accommodation is open to improvement, it is true, but the kindness and attention of mine host and hostess at the hotel " Matucana" were most grateful, and the warm yet bracing air, and ferns and flowers of the neighbourhood, make the village well worthy of a few days' rest.

Besides, when about to ascend still higher into the Cordillera for the first time, it is well to pause here for a space and accustom oneself to the rarefied air of the altitude. Matucana stands at 7788 feet above the level of the sea, and the inevitable *plaza*, fountain, church, and schools are to be found there. A few shops, containing the absolute necessities of life, an *acequia*, or running stream, coursing its way through the principal street, and an adjacent cemetery are other objects of interest; while the golden. silver, maiden-hair, and other rare and exquisite ferns, heliotrope bushes, and a variety of bright-coloured flowers enhance the beauty of the neighhood. On account of its bracing climate Matucana is much frequented by invalids, although at the time of our first visit there it was a difficult matter for them to accomplish the journey from San Bartolomé otherwise than in a litter.

In the fertile valleys of the Rimac lucerne or *alfalfa* is extensively grown as food for cattle, and the primitive mode of turning the soil by the aid of oxen yoked to a plough reminded me most forcibly of those highly coloured Biblical pictures of nursery notoriety.

Once more setting out on our faithful beasts and following the course of the rapid stream, which receives its name Rimac from the idol of oracular fame, the next obstruction was at Viso Bridge, then under repair, and presenting serious difficulties to mules and riders. Finally, the animals were induced to descend the almost perpendicular bank alone, and flounder through the river, when we quickly followed, and remounting, pursued our way up rugged zigzag paths, along the railroad track, or across the boiling river on slender osier bridges to San Mateo, where we breakfasted at the most unsavoury looking Chinese restaurant it has ever been my lot to enter.

These hanging osier bridges are frequent in the Cordillera, and are constructed of osier withes twisted into strong cables and attached to blocks of masonry, or to the natural rock, on either side of the stream ; while across the cables planks are laid, and a passage thus afforded on a swinging bridge, sometimes hundreds of feet above the abyss, although happily we were not called upon to attempt such lofty ones. The animals, as a rule, dislike them extremely, and can scarcely be induced to lead the way.

We were now at a height of 10,527 feet, and on quitting San Mateo our ascent became even more precipitous. At several hundred feet below the surging Rimac rolled with deafening roar over the giant boulders; and from our giddy heights where riding habits literally overhung the edges of the chasms, and where one false step would hurl us into the terrible abyss, we gazed with awe upon the grandeur of the scene. The magnitude of our surroundings, the mountain torrent dashing from above, and surmounting every obstacle in its anxiety to join the mighty ocean, the

height, the depth, were awe-inspiring
indeed, and they are scenes that time
can ne'er efface.

The Rimac, the one who speaks, is
surely a fitting name for this impatient,
headstrong river; and were its language
but intelligible to mortal ears, what tales
of buried ages should we hear! But
Puente del Infiernillo, rightly called
the "Gate of Hell," lies just ahead, and
here another stony staircase must be
climbed, where projecting rocks on one
side of our narrow pathway and a boiling
river on the other demand our care as
well as admiration; while overhead an
airy-looking iron bridge passes from
tunnel to tunnel on the Oroya line,
and seems as though suspended from the
clouds.

Still ruminating on the grandeur of

H

the scene, we jog along the track a while, and then ascend the mountain path to Chicla ere the daylight dies; and presently as dinner is discussed, with merry laugh and jest, we note the joys and perils of the day, and then retire to court our well-earned rest, accompanied by *sorroche*, for Chicla at 12,220 feet has many drawbacks too, and generally the altitude is first felt here. A headache with a weighty feeling on the brow, vomiting, and breathlessness are the usual symptoms of *sorroche*, although in its severer forms it causes fainting fits and bleeding at the nose and ears. Stout people, as a rule, succumb most readily to its attacks, and garlic and patience are the best known remedies for all. At a height of say 14,000 feet the air contains sixty per cent. less oxygen than on the coast, and consequently the lungs expand and have to perform forty per cent. more work in order to obtain the same result. During the expanding process *sorroche*, or the difficulty of breathing at high altitudes, occurs ; but after the lapse of a few days the general health is, as a rule, better in the mountains than on the coast, although it is never possible to undertake much physical exertion there, unless one chances to be Sierra born and bred.

A rigid clime envelopes Chicla, and during my four visits there heavy rain fell daily from about 2 P.M. upon the snow-clad heights around. From our Transandean hostel we look down on the present terminus of the Oroya railroad, and in the valley on the right the town of Chicla, with its long street and church, is seen. Our one-storied dwelling has its bedrooms in a long, low building close at hand, and only slightly guarded from the outside cold by a narrow balcony. Under this slender shelter Cholo Indians often creep at night time for repose, and on one occasion it was my misfortune to stumble over one when groping for the handle of my door. He did not grumble at the mishap, it is true, but at that time I was unacquainted with the gentle nature of the race, and hastened on without apology.

Between San Bartolomé and Chicla many brilliantly plumaged birds, lovely ferns, and bright coloured flowers, such as the scarlet anemone, calceolaria, nasturtium, heliotrope, lupin, etc., are noticeable, to say nothing of the numerous and gigantic cacti with blooms of yellow, white, and red.

At various awkward turns in zigzag paths our free passage was many a time and oft obstructed by llamas bearing ore and having leaders dressed in blue or scarlet caps and bells, or by mules and donkeys laden with eggs, vermicelli, minerals, or other cargoes from the interior, and then it was a matter of some moment to seize upon the surest foothold, regardless of all ceremony. Projecting rocks present a difficulty too, and an unnoticed one would quickly hurl the rider into an abyss.

But the most perilous, if not the most tedious, part of the journey was now accomplished, and dangers quickly faded from the mind as we dwelt upon the true magnificence and grandeur of the scene.

Thus is it in our life-long journey, time smoothes and oft obliterates our woes, but sheds a loving halo round our greatest joys.

On descending the Cordillera some months later by rail, we noticed that many little paths along which we threaded the river's bank had been completely washed away by recent floods.

CHAPTER II.

HAVING now attained the present termination of the railroad, I should like to dwell for a few brief moments on that stupendous undertaking. It was the creation of American genius, and was superintended by Mr Meiggs, assisted by Mr Cilley, whose death occurred, and was much regretted, during our stay in the Peruvian capital. The railroad was begun in 1870 and finished as far as Chicla in 1876, at a cost of £625,887 ; and in contemplating the work the beholder cannot fail to be struck with some at least of the difficulties incurred in boring through such solid rocks.

109

More than sixty tunnels have already
been cut, and the American, French, and
English bridges, which sometimes look as
though suspended in the air, are made of
stone and iron.   From the coast to
Chicla is one continued ascent, and so
labyrinthine is it that occasionally three
distinct railroad tracks can be seen at
once.   Along the precipices, through the
flinty tunnels, over the bridges, the
locomotive switchbacks up to Chicla, and
if it has not already done so, will ere long
pass through the Galera tunnel and reach
the summit range at a height of 15,732
feet.

The projected terminus is through
Oroya, 136 miles from Callao, to Cerro de
Pasco, the capital of Junin, and if not the
Grace Donoughmore, then surely some
other contract will, after cancelling

external debt according to the terms of
the contract of October 1889, connect it
with Amazonian commerce, and facilitate
the development of this vast region's
wealth through the medium of Pacific
waters. But progression travels slowly in
the country, and *paciencia* and *mañana*
(to-morrow) are as potent with Peruvians
as they were in former days at the court
of Spain, when Columbus, Cortés, and
even Pizarro all lingered there for a
recognition of their services.

Apart from the almost insuperable
difficulties already alluded to in connection
with the laying of the Oroya railroad,
there were others of a lamentable nature,
and resulting in the deaths of many
thousands of the workmen. Fevers,
verrugas, and falling boulders sadly deci-
mated their numbers, and it is estimated

that in the erection of Verrugas Bridge
alone 7000 lives were lost.

A low hand-car, drawn by gravity,
is now despatched from Chicla about
fifteen minutes in advance of the bi-
weekly trains to clear the line of fallen
pieces of rock, that threaten to impede
its downward course. These hand-cars
travel at the rate of about forty-five miles an
hour down steep inclines, and round such
frequent curves, that cause the uninitiated
many tightenings of the heart-strings as
they dwell upon the fact that a tiny
piece of rock, a skirt entangled in the
wheels, a dog, a cow, or any other animal
may at a moment's notice upset the toy
vehicle, and usher all its inmates down a
precipice and into eternity at one stroke ;
or at any rate involve the loss of a
cherished limb, for it is a difficult matter

to effect an instantaneous stoppage where
the gradient is so steep. Those who are
accustomed to this mode of travelling
describe it as delightful in spite of
constant breathlessness, and when descending from Chosica to Lima I confess
that I found the journey extremely
pleasant; but here the gradient is not so
steep, and the speed proportionately less.
The great essentials to safety and comfort
are a cautious and skilful driver, plenty
of warm clothing tightly tucked in, a hat
almost glued to the head, and a thick
veil if one prefers not being skinned by
the wind whilst moving with such rapid-
ity through it.

On our second journey from the Cordillera we quite expected to occupy this
flying car from Chicla, but recent acci-
dents frustrated the intention and obliged

the superintendent to deny us one : the ordinary train, however, proved equally convenient then, and I cannot say that I regretted the loss of this claim to honour and distinction.   Compulsory perils must be met, but the credit of having accomplished an *unnecessary* hazardous feat I willingly resign to those who have some lives to spare.

Leaving Chicla at an early hour nearly a week after our arrival there, we once more thread a stony path beside the river, and then the heights above, with the loathsome-looking condor hovering overhead.   Flowers and ferns are deserting us now, and lichens and Alpine growths supply their place.   But the magnificence of the Cordillera, unsurpassed in the grandeur of its scenery, entrances us afresh, and the mountains

show more verdure the higher we ascend,
although the last real tree we shall
behold for many months is snugly nest-
ling close to Chicla.

Suddenly, the village of Casapalca
bursts upon our view—an oasis indeed—
for in a well-known mining *hacienda*
there a hearty welcome greets our advent.
With what amazement, too, we gaze upon
the vast machinery at work, and all
transported there by mules! Upon the
distant hill-top an almost upright railroad
is discerned, from which a covered car
emerges laden with silver ore. Intent
on business, down the line it rushes, past
its empty upward bound companion, until
the terminus is reached, when with
wonderful precision it drops its precious
freight into a vast receptacle beneath,
and hastily resumes its upward track to

hurry down again. Machinery and
furnaces of wondrous size and heat soon
separate the metal from the ore, and
solid silver bars are the result. Within
the house hot-water pipes and heated
stoves soon thaw our frozen limbs, and
breakfast satisfies keen hunger's claim.
How pleasant is this rest! But Time,
man's enemy and friend, is on the wane,
and every hour delayed but makes the
summit crossing more inclement.

Again we wing our flight, and soon
the snow-capped heights, emerging from
their verdant base, seem closing in upon
us. The beasts, now conscious of their
homeward track, step boldly forth, and
stem the rapid streams with willing tread.
But they, too, have their troubles here,
and if not thoroughly accustomed to the
mountain air, or made to scale the

SMELTING WORKS OF CASAPALCA.

WU
LIAO

heights too rapidly, are liable to fall down suddenly with *sorroche,* after which they are seldom of much use for lengthy rides. None could have performed the journey with greater satisfaction to their riders than our own, although I somewhat distrusted the gentle appearance of the *negra* when she bolted up a solid rock with me on the approach of a workman's car, and still more when she caracoled so gracefully near the summit on having to pass dead llamas and mules (which so often strew the ground around) and left me with a broken tail-strap for the eastern descent!

Now, far ahead Mount Meiggs appears, and then the summit range is crossed amidst severest snow and sleet that stop the flow of mirth. Enveloped in our rugs, we peep around, and marvel whether

it is ever thus at 17,000 feet, when
suddenly a hut appears, and into it we
creep. The smoke is stifling here, and in
a dim and distant corner lies a fever-
stricken Indian man. *Sorroche* troubles
most of us, and the tiny doorway is soon
blocked in vain endeavours to get air.
An hour thus is passed, the storm mean-
while increasing, and nothing now remains
but to remount our saturated mules if we
would reach our mountain home ere
nightfall. Again the *ponchos* and
bufandas are produced, and then the
eastern slope is crossed in sadder, if not
wiser, mood. Even a *cemetery* fails to
arouse us now, and Huascacocha at
16,000 feet, one of the sources of the
Amazon, and all the other mountain
lakes are passed quite silently. Llamas
bearing merchandise from the interior

arc seen, the former extensive copper works of Morococha, the silver works of Tuctu, and the mines of Yanamina skirted ere a friendly *tambo* offers us a moment's shelter under its tiny porch.

The river Mantaro, or a tributary of it, next is crossed, and from a neighbouring height our lonely little home is seen, most snugly buried in the vale beneath. Its English farmhouse look and pleasant thatch were cheering to our gaze, and soon a heated stove and hearty meal revive our drooping frames.

At Chicla we had been obliged to do without *any* luggage for a day and night on account of the inability of the Cholo in attendance to get his pack mules through the water at Viso, and now, alas! we find that the sacks despatched from Lima more than a month ago, and con-

I

taining the bulk of our winter clothing and house linen, have been stolen! At length some Indians are imprisoned for the theft, and in five weeks' time the sacks are returned almost intact, and their contents need only disinfecting. New boots and shoes, fur cloaks, and gowns presented few attractions to the thieves; but art muslin curtains, some doilies, a cushion, and a tennis racquet (which had been packed by mistake, and which I always thought the Indians looked upon as an improved clothes' washer), evidently took their fancy.

How strange it is to dwell in this Andean nest with snowy Puy-Puy gazing so benignly on our solitude, and hundreds of graceful llamas browsing on the slopes around. The Cholo-Indian dwellers in the few surrounding huts look kindly

on us as they murmur Quichua blessings,
and the children soon become our little
friends, and run and join us in our walks.
The mornings, as a rule, are sunshiny
and bright, and then these stately walks
occur, for Nature does not give us oxygen
enough at 14,300 feet to make much
haste in anything. At one o'clock, or
later, hail, snow, or rain falls daily, and
then the turf-filled stoves invite our
presence and our mental growth, until
approaching night brings forth the cosy
chat and social hour at wanderers' return
from distant mines; and thus our days
are passed, varied sometimes with rides,
photography, or watching the process of
assaying metals. Telephones, too, were
erected during our visit to the mountains,
and connect the *hacienda* with its chief
mines. I mention this fact because I do

not imagine that any other telephones in good working order can be found at 16,000 feet above the ocean level.

A sudden change of climate next occurs, and at the close of the November month a fortnight's Indian summer cheers our hearts, and motions us to spend a dreamy hour upon the river's bank.

The frequent heavy rains in the Cordillera have already been alluded to. They are caused by evaporation from the Pacific, and the mountain streams fed by them supply the rivers flowing into the Atlantic, hence this ocean is supplied with water from the Pacific.

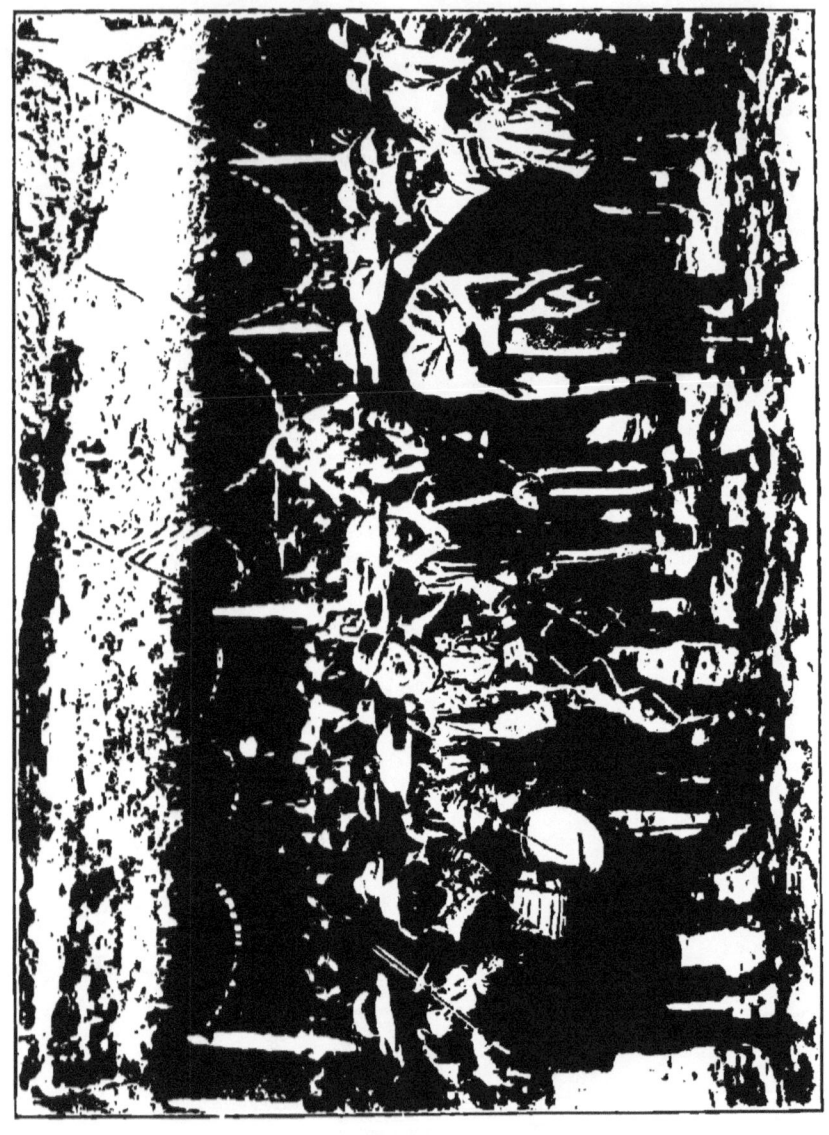

CHRISTMAS FESTIVITIES AMONGST THE CHOLO INDIANS.

CHAPTER III.

AT Christmastide a half-religious, half-secular festival was observed by the Cholo-Indians, who formerly spoke pure Quichua, the court language of the eleventh century, and quite distinct from the ancient Chimu of the coast, but have now mixed up Spanish with their own vocabulary. The Tarma band of drums and cornets was then in great request, and night as well as day the native dances flowed, while *yarabis*, Indian love songs, sounded weird and sad with strains from the guitar. In clowns' patched

127

clothes and hideous masks some dozen Cholos took the lead, and entertained beholders with a merry dance or speech, allowing little pause for rest. A *cura* next arrived, and masses, marriages, and baptisms were held at a considerable expense, while festoons of ' real flowers from Tarma and varie-coloured papers adorned the church, and all the saints were washed and renovated for the feast. Curious indeed were many of the customs observed at the Yule-tide feast by this usually melancholy race, whose chief characteristics are an apathetic demeanour and absence of expression, and the comical way in which the *cura* was escorted to and from church by maskers as he quietly lit and smoked a cigarette was not the *least* interesting feature of the week. *Chicha*, already noticed, and *chacta*, an intoxicant made from molasses, are freely—too freely—partaken of by the Cholos now and at all times; and as the women were engaged in boiling the former in earthen pots called *hoyas* outside the huts, a merry dance took place around the fires.

Bull fights were a prominent feature in the festivities too, when great dexterity was exercised by Serranos in throwing the *poncho* and screening themselves from attack, to say nothing of the pluck of the women, who fearlessly rushed into the *patio* and dragged their husbands from the scene of action. Fireworks and Chinese lanterns were displayed there also, although the former were usually discharged in broad daylight. In fact, a general "goodwill" pervaded the race, and often were we the objects of their

friendly embrace, a ceremony most
unwelcome to our cleanly natures on
account of their ignorance of, or anti-
pathy to, the use of soap !

It was no unusual thing, even in the
church, for women to rise from their
knees, kiss our hands, and then return
to prayer. This Christmas was said to
be the gayest held there for many years,
and likely to be handed down to Indian
posterity as worthy of remembrance.

The Indians have the character of
pilfering; but after once stealing our
clothes, it never seems to have occurred
to them to rob us further, and although
the front door was generally left unlocked
during the night, and the sitting room
easy of access, we never missed anything
but a door-mat from the house.

The style of dress is picturesque in

many parts of the Sierra, and here the women wear a country-woven skirt, a gaily-coloured woollen square, sometimes fastened across the chest with a large-headed silver pin, a broad felt hat, and ordinary leather boots or bullock hide shoes fastened with plaited woollen thongs. Their skin is very dark, and their long, straight glossy hair is parted down the back, and hangs in two long plaits or braids.

The chief anxiety of the men seems centred in their hose, and frequently may they be seen wearing two or even three knitted pairs at the same time. A kind of knickerbocker costume meets the hose, and shoes of bullock hide protect the feet, while nearly every Cholo sports a llama *poncho*, often brightly striped, and broad felt hat. Their eyes and skin are dark, and unkempt hair and curious little tufts arranged about the ears increase the usual mournfulness of countenance. Chewing his coca leaves, he saunters along, and with a small supply of it mixed with lime can do without a meal sometimes for days together. A beverage similar to tea is made from coca too, and proves most stimulating and sustaining to the mountain traveller, as we often found. Under the name of cocaine this plant is known in Europe as a valuable anæsthetic, and in the time of the Incas so highly was it prized that the coca trees were reserved for their special use. It is obtained from the *Erythroxylon*, which resembles the tea-shrub, and grows in sheltered places about six thousand feet above the sea. The tree often attains six feet in height, and has bright,

GROUP OF LLAMAS.

green leaves and white blossoms, which afterwards develop into red berries.

Hundreds of stately llamas dot the valleys and the mountain slopes, while frequently their outline may be seen on some high, airy cliff apparently quite near the sky. And a pretty sight it is to see them gazing shyly round as they march along in droves laden with sacks containing precious ore. About 100 lbs. each carries; and should the *chaconia* who lades them attempt to put much greater weight, they doggedly refuse to move until relieved of part.

Before visiting the country I had read a great deal about the affection of the *arriero* for his llamas, and understood that he frequently knelt down beside them and with endearing terms coaxed them to arise. This must have been in bygone ages, for *prods* are used now, and the Cholo of the present day treats his llamas somewhat after the same style as his ancestors were treated by their Spanish conquerors. Llamas vary both in shade and colour, but dark brown ones with black head and feet are generally the most admired. The coarse *ychu* grass, growing in tufts upon the mountain slopes, is all the food they need, and for the transportation of ore and merchandise they are invaluable, males only being worked. A curious fact connected with them is that after nightfall, even though they may just have arrived from a whole day's journey, they will take no food until the dawn.

Time passes quickly here, and many pleasant rides on horses and on mules we take, where red auriferous heights

MOUNTAIN SCENERY, SHOWING THE RIVER MANTARO.

with snowy peaks beneath a glaring sun demand our warmest admiration; or again, where giant icicles bespeak the frigid atmosphere.

Yauli, the postal town, is about two leagues away, and has warm mineral springs that contain the same curative properties as the European ones of Carlsbad. On our first visit to this town we formed a curious company I own, one lady being mounted on a horse that pirouetted gaily for half an hour in his amazement at seeing a riding habit for the first time, our Peruvian escort bestriding a mule that never ceased kicking for two minutes together, and I myself exerting all my strength to check a powerful and frisky mule that had not been exercised for nearly a week!

But Yauli, and the neighbouring

Pachachaca, show signs of war's destructive power in roofless, ruined houses, for the Chilians penetrated even here, and a force of five thousand men reached Tarma and even Jauja beyond. As elsewhere in the mountains, *adobe*, sun-dried bricks, are used for walls, and thatch, or corrugated iron, kept in place by weighty stones, supplies a roof.

The famous Chanchamayo valley, with its fruitful crops and genial clime, Tarma, Huancayo, and Jauja, the haven of consumptives, all lie within a few days' ride on mule-back from us, and welcome foreign residents. Much beautiful silver filigree work, too, is done at Huancayo, Cerro de Pasco, and other places in the interior; and from the wool of the llama, vicuña, huanaco, and alpaca *ponchos*, *bufandas*, blankets, and rugs are made,

while the rabbit-like chinchilla supplies
the fur so greatly prized in Europe.
The Mantaro, or Oroya, is the only river
of importance in the district, and its
affluents wind serpent-like throughout the
Yauli valley.

Biscaches, animals resembling rab-
bits in appearance and taste, wild
geese, ducks, teal, and other water-fowl
abound, and smaller birds are often seen
as well. The gloomy-looking condor flies
far o'erhead, eager for his prey, and
presently swoops down to feast upon the
carrion near, so quickly sighted by his
piercing glance.

Cattle, sheep, the native horse and
mule, can live here well, but donkeys,
goats, domestic fowl, soon suffer from
the altitude and die.

On the mining statistics of Peru it is

not my purpose to enlarge; that has already been done, and will again be attempted, by an abler pen than mine, as the flow of European emigration to this Western storehouse increases.

All native and foreign residents in the Sierra are engaged in some way or other with mining interests, and even casual visitors become enthusiastic over ores displayed.

No trees nor vegetables take root in this ungenial clime, and yet a restful verdure clothes the country round, and tiny little flowers with stalks not half an inch in height, the low-growing cactus with its yellow flowers, and a few hardy ferns proclaim that Flora deigns to visit even this lone, lofty spot. Indeed, it was while prowling round alone in quest of ferns one day that my head became wedged between two rocks. The coveted specimen lay far back, and in order to reach it I was obliged to stretch myself on the ground and insert my head and hand.

The entrance was easy enough, and the fern grasped, but how to withdraw myself again was quite another matter. Wriggle as I would, my head would not come out, and I was beginning to think seriously and fearfully of my horrible fate, and wondering whether it could possibly have increased in size since it entered there, when a lucky twist released me. This was my last experience of fern-gathering amongst the rocks, and henceforth I gladly left them for other hands to pluck!

The waterfall of Puy-Puy is one of the grandest sights within a day's ride of us,

K

and it fairly dazzles the beholder with its wondrous grace and beauty as it glistens in the morning sun.   At the base of an ever snowclad point (19,000 feet) this waterfall, of seven parts, at 16,800 feet above the sea, forms one of the sources of the mighty Amazon, and is approached by narrow, rocky pathways, where in one place the mules' heads are seen round one side of a projecting rock, while their tails remain on the other, so narrow and winding is the path.   At the waterfall we held a birthday picnic, and so scorching was the sun that we gladly retired to the rocks for shelter.   Potted meats, sardines, eggs, wine, beer, and every Sierra luxury were displayed—the bread alone was missing!—and a very pleasant day was passed; but on returning to our home at four o'clock, we found deep snow around, thus quickly does our climate change.

A few months' bracing mountain air, and then a journey to the coast once more, o'er snow and ice that make the beasts walk warily, and tax our utmost strength and watchfulness in keeping up at all. Such weather has not been for many years, and our progression is but slow across the bleak and pathless summit to the town of Chicla. Coloured glasses somewhat shield our eyesight from the glare, but nothing saves our faces from the cold. For nine long hours we ride, and then with faces skinned and limbs benumbed, despite the welcome halt at Casapalca, seek shelter for the night, and quit familiar Chicla by the morning train bound for the coast.

CHAPTER IV.

To say that we enjoyed a return to warmth would but slightly convey the joy experienced; and even the five long hours at Verrugas Bridge, under a scorching sun, were not unbearable, although so sudden a change of climate sorely tried our constitutions; and on seeing the tiny car pitch like a vessel at sea, or a swinging boat at a fair, I decided upon leaving my friends to cross the bridge alone, and performed my transit by the steep and lengthy valley path instead. But the alternative was an arduous and risky exploit; and had it not been for the ready help afforded by the

146

Chilian and Peruvian who attended me, and carried me over the widest jumps, my mangled remains would certainly have been left below for the condors' investigation.

Weary, sick, and faint, and with the lament of old Gobbo's son, " When I shun Scylla your father, I fall into Charybdis your mother," ringing in mine ears, the next few hours are passed, until the locomotive takes us to Chosica, where old acquaintances look strangely on our much discoloured faces, and disconcert us by their askant looks, as though they greeted visitants from other worlds. Evidently when they said *adios* so affectionately some months ago they *meant* it, and our reappearance quite takes them by surprise. The idea is gruesome, but we weather it, and the next day journey on a hand-car down to Lima. Undoubtedly it was wise to enter the capital in an unpretentious hand-car instead of in the ordinary train, as our main object now was to escape the public gaze, and hide mahogany physiognomics for a while until the skinning process should be over. But wan and ghastly all our former friends appear, and their pallor wakes a vein of pity in our bosoms as they call to greet us back. *They*, surely, must be greatly changed, or *we*.

The heat is now intense, and Guayaquil hammocks but enhance a *dolce far niente* life, until the Carnival comes round and renders every spot unsafe, and even trusty friends' vicinity suspicious; while an opera season and the city's gaieties are truly grateful after some months' seclusion in the lofty Cordillera; for man is of a gregarious nature, after all, despite dyspeptic utterances of poets and philosophers.

A sojourn at the sea is next proposed, and soon we are established at Barranco, not half an hour by train from Lima, and walk on to the flat roof of the curiously built hotel on emerging from our rooms. A charming public avenue, beneath a trellis-work of vines, conducts us to the bathing-place, and rocky banks and caves are, as at Miraflores, covered and lined with maiden-hair fern, through which a constant stream is seen to gently percolate. But strictly primitive the bathing is, and whites and blacks all take their dip together, and battle with the waves in unison.

Mindful of many warnings from residents, and of the unpleasant circumstance of being followed by a ruffian when exploring Lima's outskirts, I now endeavoured to restrict my walks to parts inhabited; but one day wandered on until the battlefield of Miraflores lay before me, and sorrowfully I dwelt on scenes enacted there in 1881 between two nations who but yesterday boasted of one common brotherhood, and, in a practically cival war, so rudely trampled on the sacred ties of ancestry and kindred.

At Ancon, La Punta, Chorrillos, Barranco, or Miraflores, the well-to-do inhabitants of Lima may generally be found during the capital's most enervating seasons.

Again we journey to our mountain home, travelling by the train this time as far as Chicla, and crossing dread Verrugas in the car suspended from a

chain—a better mode by far than that
employed by workmen, who are slung
over on a board without sides, and often
have not space for both feet on the plank,
as with iron grip their hands close on the
chains above. No unknown terrors now
to mar our upward flight; and the very
elements, as though to compensate for
former wrongs, suspend their fury for
a while, and disclose fresh beauties in the
distant cañons, or in snowy peaks that
seem to pierce the sky.

Amongst the Indian race a curious
custom still prevails of wearing mourning
for the Inca, killed in 1533; though
whether they don it to commemorate any
circumstance connected with that monarch,
or only when their immediate surroundings are distasteful, I was unable to
ascertain. The women wear a black

gown with broad, brightly - flowered border; and on the only occasion when a mourner came beneath my notice, it seemed to have been put on with special reference to a departing priest, who, judging by the frantic efforts made by his followers to drag him through the carriage window, must have been taking with him all their hopes of future bliss as well as present solace.

A few weeks later still, and Lima welcomes us again, but only for *adieux*. The year, with all its strange experiences, has quickly flown, and as farewells are said, two strangely different sorrows fill my heart. The one, that some of our number remain behind; the other, that that ancient capital of Cuzco has not been seen. Ruins are, it is true, its chief characteristics now, but all our memories

of ancient Incas cling to the spot; and, if
we may credit the writings of Sarmiento
who visited it in 1550, and gleaned his
information from the natives, "neither in
Jerusalem, Rome, nor Persia, nor in any
other part of the world, was there ever
collected in one place such a profuse
magnificence of treasure in gold, silver,
and jewels, as at this place Cuzco." We
know, moreover, that its large stone
temple of the Sun, and many other buildings, excited the keenest admiration of
the Spanish conquerors, and that the
bulk of Atahualpa's ransom was collected
here—a ransom, alas! that failed to free
him from the terrible garrote at the
hands of his faithless enemies on August
29, 1533. But Cuzco was too far off,
and would have entailed a voyage to
Mollendo, and then a tedious inland

journey towards the shores of famous Titicaca, so perforce remained unvisited.

"Adieu, thou hospitable and sunny land! May peace at home protect thee, and success abroad attend thee, until thine ancient splendor greet thee."

With a goodly company on board, and the usual complement of cosmopolitan adventurers and priests, the stately vessel skims the ocean fair, beneath a scorching sun, onward to Panamá. A veritable Lethe this, where the business man forgets his sordid cares, the sorrowful his woes, and only Muses and the merry god are welcomed in our midst. "Enchanting Nature! thy beauty is not only in heaven and earth, but in the waters under our feet."

Again the arid Paita coast-line looms ahead; but on hearing that the interior is green and fertile, and that a corpse had to be decoyed from Panamá to quiet the superstition respecting an untenanted cemetery, we are somewhat comforted concerning the welfare of the compulsory residents there.

No Isthmian reptiles to molest us now. Our temporary home is on the Bay of Panamá, and varied by stray shots at sharks, a picnic to an island near, and struggles after orchids, until the train transports us to Colon to join that ancient *s.s.* of the same cognomen bound for New York. No calm Pacific waters these, and the rough Carribbean grants no knowledge of the many passengers, amongst whom curious Californian specimens are ranged, until King Neptune's wrath is spent, and Heaven's artillery is heard no more.

The island of Navassa next appears, whose rigorous laws permit no woman to approach its shores, and Cuba and other West Indian Islands soon are sighted, before Cape Hatteras is passed, and the lights of Barnegat denote our nearness to the port. On the following morn we ride at anchor off Staten Island, and get a near view of the colossal statue of Liberty, so full of meaning to the sons and daughters of the *free*. But harmony is here invaded by the Custom House Inquisitor, whose chief business seems to consist in finding out how many travellers speak the truth, inasmuch as they are first of all requested to swear on oath that they possess no contrabands, and are then subjected to a *searching* test on the New York wharf.

How widely different is this city's

bustle to the *mañana* and "at your disposition" of Peruvians, who place, by word of mouth, their house and all its contents at the "disposition" of their casual acquaintances! The phrase is neatly turned, though meaningless, and what might happen if an unsuspicious foreigner should take them at their word is a problem difficult to solve.

Amongst Peruvians, too, it is *infra dignitatem* for a woman to support herself by exercising brain or hand, and many a man is sorely pinched through housing his spinster sisters, and his cousins and his aunts; but here, in this vast city, even more than in England itself, the women take their stand beside the men in the battle-field of life, and hasten to their daily avocations.

How stirring is the giant capital, and

with what eager eyes I gaze upon its "lions" in my too brief stay! Although with the thermometer at 103° Fahrenheit, sight-seeing is somewhat arduous, despite the frequent "lifts." Broadway, Fifth Avenue, the Elevated Railroad, Central Park, and Brooklyn Bridge seem visited in dreams, before the city's namesake of the Inman Line quits Sandy Hook, and with herculean respiration bears its international freight of pleasure-seekers and hard workers towards that "precious stone set in the silver sea."

THE END.

Printed at THE EDINBURGH PRESS, *9 and 11 Young Street.*

www.ingramcontent.com/pod-product-compliance
Lightning Source LLC
Chambersburg PA
CBHW031113020726
47495CB00007B/2180